I See
You See

I See
You See

Richard Jackson

Illustrated by Patrice Barton

A Caitlyn Dlouhy Book

Atheneum Books for Young Readers

New York   London   Toronto   Sydney   New Delhi

ATHENEUM BOOKS FOR YOUNG READERS

An imprint of Simon & Schuster Children's Publishing Division

1230 Avenue of the Americas, New York, New York 10020

Text © 2021 by the Estate of Richard Jackson

Illustrations © 2021 by Patrice Barton

Book design by Greg Stadnyk © 2021 by Simon & Schuster, Inc.

ATHENEUM BOOKS FOR YOUNG READERS is a registered trademark of Simon & Schuster, Inc. Atheneum logo is a trademark of Simon & Schuster, Inc.

For information about special discounts for bulk purchases, please contact Simon & Schuster Special Sales at 1-866-506-1949 or business@simonandschuster.com.

The Simon & Schuster Speakers Bureau can bring authors to your live event. For more information or to book an event, contact the Simon & Schuster Speakers Bureau at 1-866-248-3049 or visit our website at www.simonspeakers.com.

The text for this book was set in 1786 GLC Fournier.

The illustrations for this book were rendered in pencil sketches and mixed media, and assembled and painted digitally.

Manufactured in China

1120 SCP

First Edition

10 9 8 7 6 5 4 3 2 1

Library of Congress Cataloging-in-Publication Data

Names: Jackson, Richard, 1935–2019 author. | Barton, Patrice, 1955– illustrator.

Title: I see you see / Richard Jackson ; illustrated by Patrice Barton.

Description: New York : Atheneum, [2021] | Summary: Jonah tags along when Maise takes the dog, Tinker, out, and he turns their walk into an exercise in imagination.

Identifiers: LCCN 2019017840 | ISBN 9781481492003 (hardcover) | ISBN 9781481492010 (eBook)

Subjects: | CYAC: Imagination—Fiction. | Brothers and sisters—Fiction. | Neighborhoods—Fiction.

Classification: LCC PZ7.1.J35 Ias 2021 | DDC [E]—dc23

LC record available at https://lccn.loc.gov/2019017840

To my extraordinary sister, Janie, with love

–P. B.

Mom calls, "Maisie, walk the dog, will you?"

"Me too," Jonah says to his sister.

"Walk me."

"Oh, brother," Maisie mutters, snapping on Tinker's leash.

"Not you, Jonah. I didn't mean you. It's this silly dog. Stay, Tink."

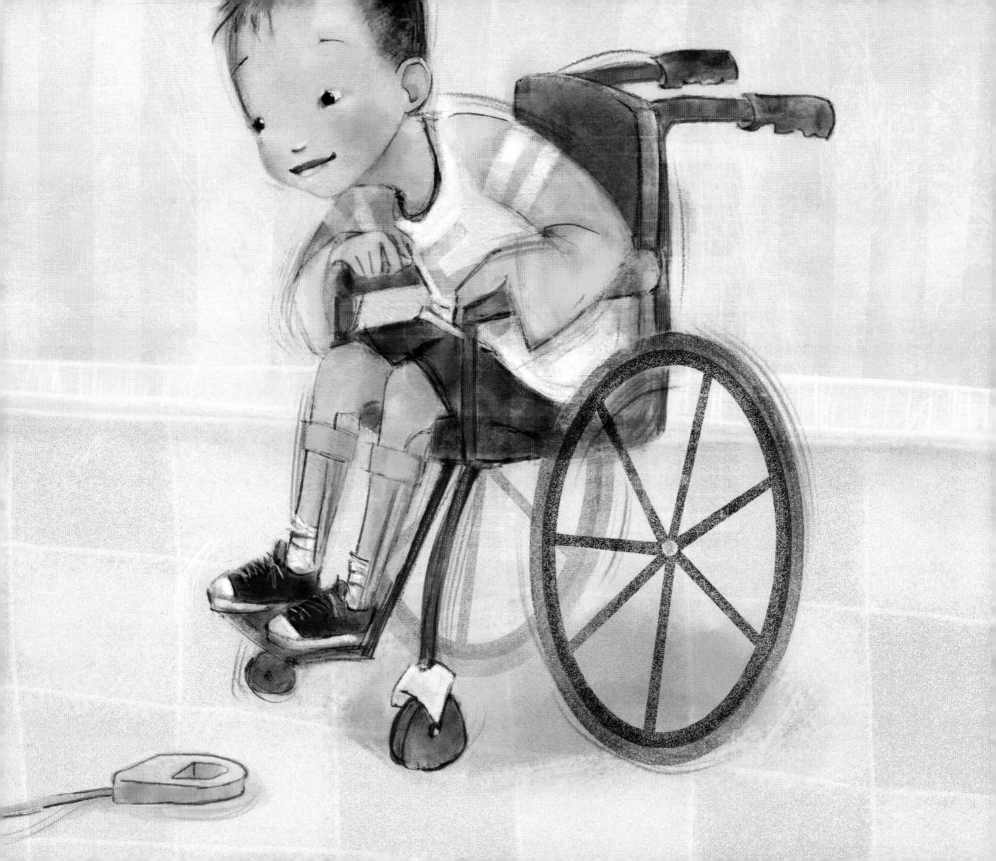

Dog pulling,
Maisie pushing,
they set off.

Woof-woof—woofwoofwoof

before they even get to the corner.

"TINKER!"

"Look, Maisie. A tree of cats . . .

"A Popsicle garden."

Woooof.

"A sky slide . . .

See?"

"I see Mr. Siegel, waving."

"And there, a tingly tunnel—

damp, echo-y-y-y-y-y."

"Now Tink is all tangled. . . ."

"Oh look . . .

. . . a bell machine!"

"I hear it, I think."

"Ting-a-ling, jingle . . .
B_ong, b_ong, b_ong.

"A hula of hoops, loop-the-looping."

"Tink, *no.*"

"Lapping up soup . . ."
Jonah laughs.

"Baby dinos . . ."

"Look, they're on stilts!" Maisie pointed.

"They see me, the dinos.
They wag their tails—*hello, hello* . . .
They know me . . . from yesterday,
yesterday, tomorrow.
Yes. Today."

"Look, Jonah.

Back where we started . . .

at the cat tree."

Woofwoof!

"Who does he see?

The cats or . . .

Mr. Siegel?"

"Oh, the goldfish . . .